Edge of Disaster

John Parker

Scholastic Canada Ltd.

Copyright © 2001 Scholastic Canada Ltd.
By arrangement with Sundance Publishing

All rights reserved. No part of this publication may be
reproduced, stored in a retrieval system or transmitted
in any form or by any means, electronic, mechanical,
photocopying, recording, or otherwise, without the prior
written permission of the publisher.

Published by Scholastic Canada Ltd.
175 Hillmount Road, Markham, ON L6C 1Z7

Copyright © 2000 Sundance Publishing
Copyright © text John Parker

First published 1999 as Phenomena by
Horwitz Martin
A Division of Horwitz Publications Pty Ltd
55 Chandos St., St. Leonards NSW 2065 Australia

ISBN 978-0-7791-1010-0

Printed in Canada

10 9 8 7 6 5 4   07 08 09 10 11

Contents

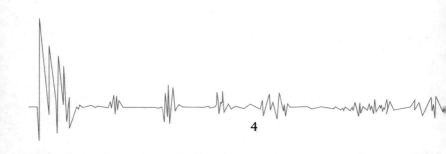

4

Author's Note

In every natural disaster, there are stories of people like you and me—and maybe the person sitting next to you in class. They are people who somehow face destruction and tragedy with bravery and determination. I find those stories important and inspiring.

Though I've never been in a natural disaster, I just missed being on Ruapehu (Roo-a-pay-ho) when it erupted. I had been skiing on the mountain just two days before it blew up and saw the steam shooting from the crater lake. A few days later, I was in a plane that passed close to the huge black clouds spurting from the crater.

Since giving up teaching to become a full-time author, John Parker has written over seventy books for children and young adults. When he's not writing, John likes to ski and hike.

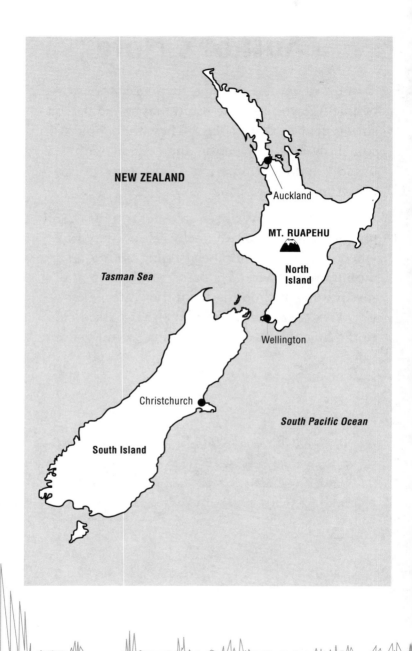

NEW ZEALAND

Auckland

MT. RUAPEHU

North
Island

Tasman Sea

Wellington

Christchurch

South Pacific Ocean

South Island

Chapter 1
Trouble at School

Fact: New Zealand is an island country about 1600 kilometres southeast of Australia. It consists of two main islands—North Island and South Island—and many smaller islands.

ABOUT TWO WEEKS after his dad left home, Darren Taylor woke up feeling as if an iron band was twisted around his chest. He couldn't breathe properly. He couldn't think clearly. He couldn't eat his breakfast. And when he left for school, he slammed the door without saying goodbye to his mom.

At school, he couldn't concentrate during Mr. Fisher's geography class. It was worse in math after the morning break. He usually enjoyed math and looked forward to Mr. Gulliver's jokes. But he couldn't keep his mind on the lesson today.

He had his eyes half-shut, trying to make it through until the lunch bell, when Mr. Gulliver spoke. "Zap through this question, Darren."

Darren's aching head tried to make sense of the figures. "Come on, Darren," cracked Mr. Gulliver. "I've 'Taylored' this question just for you." As the class laughed, Darren felt like he would explode.

Brett Rowe, who sat behind Darren, laughed loudly. Then he put his hand under his desk and prodded Darren in the back. "Dumb Darren," he whispered.

Something snapped in Darren's brain. He whirled around and grabbed Brett. "Hey!" yelped Brett in surprise, clutching the edge of his desk. Brett and the desk crashed to the floor.

Mr. Gulliver's cheerful expression disappeared. "Stop!" he thundered. But Darren heard nothing except the roaring in his head. He thumped his knees down on Brett's chest and pushed Brett's head down as hard as he could against the floor.

Brett opened his mouth to say something. Darren wanted to crunch that mouth that had jeered at him. He lifted his arm as high as he could. But before he could hit Brett, Mr. Gulliver held Darren's arm in a grip of steel. He yanked him up. "On your feet, young man!"

When Darren stood up, his legs shook so much he almost fell over. The class stared at him in amazement. Darren felt like crying.

That afternoon, Darren was sitting in the principal's office, his mom and dad on either side. Darren tried looking at the big books lining the walls. Then decided to stare at the dark green carpet.

His mom explained that there were some problems at home that had led to Darren's behaviour. She told Mrs. Ramsey that she was sure Darren would never do anything like that again.

Mrs. Ramsey looked over the top of her glasses at Darren, who kept his eyes on the floor. "Is your mother correct, young man?" she asked.

"Yes, Mrs. Ramsey," Darren mumbled.

Then his dad interrupted loudly. "If you and the rest of the staff in this lousy school can't keep control, then you should start digging ditches instead."

He got up with a sarcastic "Excuse me." He banged the door on his way out. A few seconds later, they heard his big car speed off with a squeal of tires.

Darren's mom closed her eyes. Darren's chest felt tight again. In the silence, he heard the ticking clock on the principal's desk.

Mrs. Ramsey asked Darren to wait outside. Ten minutes later, his mom came out. They drove home in silence.

"Mrs. Ramsey thinks it's a good idea for you to stay away from school until things have settled down," his mom finally said. Darren shrugged his shoulders. "Would you like to go anywhere?"

Darren shrugged his shoulders again. Then he remembered a promise his dad had made a few weeks ago. "Dad said he'd take me skiing." But when Darren phoned his dad that night, his dad said he was too busy. Maybe in a few weeks.

Darren's mom wasn't surprised. "What your father says and what he does are two different things."

Darren went to his room and flopped on the bed. An hour later, his mom knocked on the door, smiling.

"It's all set. We're going to New Zealand. We can stay at your aunt's motel at Ruapehu. She'll set you up for free ski lessons for three days. Happy?"

"New Zealand? Are you kidding?" Darren asked.

"Well, I got a really low fare and I've been planning to visit your grandparents for months. It's been so long since you've seen everyone. I think this is just the break we both need."

Darren wasn't so sure. It had been three years since he'd been to New Zealand. Besides, he wanted to learn to ski with his dad, not on his own. But he had to think of his mom. She always talked about how much she missed her family, especially since Dad had left.

"Okay. When do we leave?"

Ten days later, Darren waited on the side of the road beside the Topview Motor Inn for the ski shuttle. His ski boots felt like boulders tied to his feet. His skis and poles were hard to hold. His ski hat was too tight. The strap on his fanny pack was loose. He wanted to throw it away even though it held his sunscreen and a chocolate bar.

The ski shuttle arrived in a smelly cloud of diesel fumes. Its tires crunched the gravel on the side of the road. As Darren clumped up the bus steps with his skis, the driver stopped him.

"Hey, mate! Skis on the racks!" The driver heaved himself from behind the wheel and thumped down the steps. He wore an enormous yellow shirt that stretched to his knees. His thick hair was tied in a knot at the back. His face hadn't seen a razor for days.

"Round the back, mate." He took Darren's skis and casually slotted them into the racks on the end of the bus. "First time at the mountain?" he asked. Darren nodded. "Wouldn't catch this Maori skiing," he grinned, as the bus lurched into action. "Too cold. But my daughter works up there. She's crazy, eh?"

The shuttle chugged up the road. The high trees soon gave way to small scrub trees. The whole view had been shaped by the rising mountain and years of bending to the wind. Tufts of grass clung to patches of soil. Clumps of snow grew bigger until snow ran in an unbroken white line beside the road.

The shuttle stopped outside a luxury hotel. The skiers boarding from the hotel wore jackets in the latest colours, movie-star sunglasses, and shiny new boots. Darren tried to hide his old rented boots and the cracked goggles his mom had dug out of the closet. The hotel skiers talked another language— The Valley,

Maori: Native peoples of New Zealand.

The Knoll, The Pinnacles. He felt like a fish on land.

Or more like a fish on a bumpy bus to a mountain he couldn't see, on a vacation he didn't want. As for the Topview Motor Inn, it was a stupid name to call a place where you couldn't see the mountain through the clouds.

The shuttle climbed more steeply, grinding upward in first gear. The snow was now thick and solid, piled against the wheels of the parked cars and the walls of the ski lodges. It was colder. Darren pulled his wool hat down over his ears.

The shuttle jerked to a halt. He clambered out, pulled out his skis, then looked around for the ski school. It was about sixty metres feet above him in the mist. But as he started up the slope, his boots slipped on an icy patch. He fell over, his skis clattering to the ground.

Someone picked them up for him. "You'll need these." A strong-looking woman handed them to Darren. She wore a blue and black ski suit with a red badge on it. It said: 'Andrea: Ski Patrol.'

"Easy to fall," she said. "I've done it, too. Dig the front edges of your boots into the snow when

> *The Valley, The Knoll, The Pinnacles:* Names of the ski fields on the mountain.

you're going uphill." Suddenly she thrust out a hand. "That'll be five dollars."

Darren's mouth dropped. You had to pay for advice from the ski patrol! Five dollars was all he had for lunch. He fished in his jacket pocket for the money.

"Hey, just kidding," said Andrea. Her white teeth flashed with amusement. "Say, what's your name?"

"Darren."

"First time on the mountain?" asked Andrea.

"First and last," said Darren, sourly.

"Hey!" said Andrea. "Be positive! Everyone has a first day. Having a lesson?"

Darren nodded.

"That's good," said Andrea. "It'll start you off doing things right. You'll love it."

Darren remembered the words of the shuttle driver. "The guy who drove me here in the shuttle thought skiing was crazy."

Andrea threw her head back and laughed. She tossed the words over her shoulder as she walked up the hill. "He's my father. Don't listen to him. One day, I'll get him on skis. Skiing's magic."

Skiing's magic. The same words the ski mechanic

had said when he fitted me for boots and skis last night, thought Darren. He could still smell the hot wax in the fitting room as the ski mechanic worked on the skis. Around the walls, skis and poles were hung in racks. He remembered how he had to wriggle his feet into the tight boots that made you lean forward. And the sharp snap as he stamped his boots into the bindings. But magic? No way!

Darren found his way to the ski school through the crowds of skiers, and showed his receipt to the woman at the ticket window. She spoke to someone behind her.

A few seconds later a tall man walked out. He wore the orange and blue jacket of the ski school. His face was deeply tanned except for white patches around his eyes where his goggles sat.

The man shook Darren's hand. "Hi, Darren." He had an American accent. "I'm Pete. We'll be skiing very soon—but first we need two other kids."

He read from a piece of paper, "Yoshi Yamada?" A small, stocky Japanese boy came forward and introduced himself. He had a serious face and short black hair. He smiled at Pete, who shook his hand. Then he nodded shyly at Darren.

> **bindings**: *Clamps that attach the ski boots to the ski.*

Pete looked at his paper again. "Kelly? Kelly Gale?" A tall girl with red-brown hair rushed up so quickly she bumped into him. The words tumbled out as she made her excuses.

"Sorry I'm late. We only got into Taupo this morning. Then Mom couldn't get the car to start. I'll probably be late for my own funeral!" She fumbled in the pocket of her expensive red ski jacket and showed Pete the receipt for the ski class.

When Pete introduced himself, she burst out laughing at his goggle marks. "Wow! You look like a panda!" She put her hand over her mouth. "Sorry. My mom always tells me to think before I talk."

Pete didn't mind. "Follow the panda," he laughed. "Let's go to Happy Valley and see what this skiing thing is all about."

Darren grappled with his skis as if they were slippery eels. "Hey!" said Pete. "Lesson number one—how to carry the darn things."

He placed his skis face to face, clicked the binding brakes together, and put them on his shoulder front end down, tails up. It looked easy.

"Your turn," he said to Darren. Darren copied what Pete had done. The skis were balanced securely on his shoulder.

"Great!" said Pete. "Now you're beginning to look like a real skier." Darren couldn't help feeling satisfied. He liked doing things the right way. It was like math—if you did it right, you got it right.

Pete led them to a small chairlift that ran down to Happy Valley, alongside a back wall of jagged rock. Pete pointed to it. "Lava flows," he said.

"Lava flows!" exclaimed Kelly. "So we're skiing on something that'll sizzle and explode!" She sounded excited. "Don't tell Mom. She'll have a fit."

"Welcome to Mt. Ruapehu and the volcanic plateau," said Pete. "Sorry to disappoint you, Kelly. These lava flows could be ten thousand years old. And this old mound of snow hasn't erupted for years and years, way back before you were born."

lava flows: Streams of molten or hot liquid rock.

plateau: A high area of flat land.

Ruapehu (Roo-a-pay-ho)

"There's nothing as exciting as volcanoes in Sydney," said Kelly.

"So, you're from Australia," said Pete. He turned to Yoshi. "And you're from Japan." Yoshi nodded.

"Yes, I'm from Kobe," said Yoshi quietly.

"Really?" said Pete. "Were you in the earthquake?"

Yoshi said nothing.

"Is your family here?"

"My father is in Auckland, with my brother. They are here for the weekend," Yoshi said. His English was excellent. "I am staying at Ridgetop."

"Good lodge," said Pete. "Great food!"

Yoshi looked happy. "Yes!" he said. "Very good."

"And I'm told you're from Vancouver," said Pete to Darren. "Where are you staying?"

"Topview Motor Inn," said Darren.

"Well," said Pete. "I'm from a little place called West Plains in Missouri. We're sure an international bunch, aren't we?"

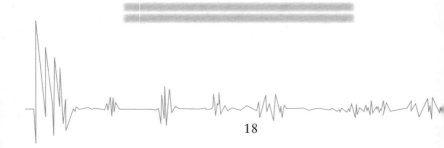

Chapter 2
Wrestle the Bear!

<u>Fact</u>: Mt. Ruapehu (pronounced Roo-a-pay-ho) is the highest mountain in the North Island of New Zealand and an active volcano. It is 2796 metres high and has three ski fields.

DARREN STUMBLED OFF the chairlift and followed the others. He noticed that Yoshi walked with a slight limp. Apart from miles of snow and the dim distant slopes, Darren could see little but mist and clammy clouds.

The mist swirled around the slopes. Darren's nose was raw and cold. His breath steamed. This is stupid, he thought. Tonight I'll tell Mom that I want to go home.

Then he saw the snow get brighter. He looked up. He could see patches of blue sky. The clouds were breaking. Mist

chairlift: Seats held by cables and used to transport people up and down mountains.

and clouds moved, then lifted, like a curtain rising on a play. The snow started to glisten in the sun. Heaps and hollows, hills and valleys, cliffs and crevices all appeared as the mountain revealed itself. The slopes rose to sharp peaks. Giant fists of black rock thrust out from the slopes. Towers of ice and snow steepled into the sky. Then Darren saw the top of the mountain. It swept across the sky. It was thrilling.

Yoshi gazed in wonder. Kelly waved her ski poles. "Wow!" she yelled. Darren took a deep breath. Pete chuckled at their reactions. "Now we know why we're here, eh?"

Then Yoshi pointed to something drifting in the sky at the top. "Steam," he said.

"Yep," said Pete. "The crater lake is hydrothermal. All the heat under the water gives it the burps. When old man Ruapehu gets his lungs hot, he has to clear his throat."

crevice: *A crack.*

hydrothermal: *Water heated by volcanic activity.*

Yoshi was concerned. "There is danger?"

"The lake's sure heating up," Pete replied. "But we're still only at a level-two alert. The science guys think Ruapehu is a little above low-eruptive activity. That means you're probably in more danger from eating your morning cereal."

Kelly was disappointed. "I want to see a live volcano! It'd be cool!" She turned to Pete. "How come you know all this?"

"I trained as a geologist—until the skiing bug took over," Pete said. He looked around at the dazzling slopes. "I'm not complaining," he said.

Pete found a flat area of snow. "Let's get used to these things," he said.

They stamped their feet into their bindings and tried walking along the snow on their skis. Kelly strode off as if she was running a race. She fell over immediately, giggling so much she couldn't get up.

Darren lost his balance, falling sideways and hitting a crusty piece of snow with his hip. It hurt. He rubbed the sore spot.

Pete helped them both up. "Everyone falls," he said. "Just relax when you go

geologist: Scientist who studies the physical history of the Earth.

down and enjoy it." But Darren didn't think a bruised hipbone was funny.

Yoshi didn't fall. He glided smoothly and solidly on his skis. "You've done this before," Pete said.

Yoshi nodded. "A little."

"Would you like to go to a higher level?" asked Pete.

"No," said Yoshi. "My father says it is good for me to learn again. I am happy."

Darren tried once more. The snow seemed a long way down from his head. Pete seemed to guess what Darren was thinking. "Ever climbed a tree in your bare feet?" he asked. Darren remembered the big oak on their neighbour's property. He always climbed it in the summer. He loved the feel of the warm bark under his toes and feet as he gripped the branches.

Darren nodded. "Then ski the same way—thinking through your feet," said Pete. Darren took his advice. When he walked around again, his skis felt part of his body, rather than alien strips of plastic tacked to his feet.

"Now it's time for a run down a hill," Pete said. "We'll start from there." He pointed to the top of a gentle slope, about twenty-seven metres up.

Kelly wagged her finger at Pete. "I've got a horrible

feeling, Panda Pete, that you're going to make us walk up there."

"Edging up a hill is a great technique," Pete said. He wrapped his arms around himself and pretended to shiver. "And we need the exercise."

They watched Pete as he set his skis sideways to the slope. Then he edged up, digging the top edge of each ski into the slope. They did the same. It was like going up stairs sideways. Darren felt his skis bite into the snow. If he edged, his skis stayed firm. He started to feel good about learning how to do it.

Darren reached the top, breathing hard. Pete was right. He was feeling warmer. He also felt hungry.

Pete turned his skis to face downhill. "Ski time! Let your skis run until they stop at the bottom. Stay forward on the skis. Have fun." Pete skied smoothly to the bottom, turned around, then waved for Kelly to begin.

Kelly swooshed down, whooping as her skis gathered speed. Then Pete waved to Darren. Darren felt the wind in his face as his skis slid down the slope. But near the bottom he got scared and let his weight fall back. Immediately the skis

edging: Walking sideways on skis to move up a hill.

shot forward from under him. He crashed.

Snow got behind his goggles and down his neck. Kelly brushed it off for him. "Great fall," she said. "Ten out of ten." Darren tried to join in her laughter, but he felt annoyed with himself for being scared.

Pete waved for Yoshi to ski down. Yoshi skied down calmly. Pete clapped his hands. "Nice work."

They tried the slope twice more. And each time Darren lost his confidence and crashed. He was getting tired of brushing off the snow. "You need a windshield wiper on your goggles," joked Kelly.

"Time to take the platter lift," Pete said. They skied to the lift line and watched Pete. He placed the platter under his legs, waited until the platter wire tightened, then slid smoothly up the slope. Kelly and Yoshi went up smoothly, too.

Darren didn't. He sat down on his platter—and fell back onto the snow. Before he could free the platter, the platter wire tightened and the platter caught his jacket, dragging him up the slope. Then the wire slipped free, dancing crazily. It wrapped around a

platter lift: A ski lift on which skiers are towed up slopes while sitting on a disc attached by a wire to a moving cable.

lift tower and tangled. The lift ground to a halt. The attendant had to climb up and unravel the wire.

The line was long by the time Darren finally made it to the top. He was embarrassed. He figured half the mountain must have seen him floundering in the snow. Pete clapped him on the shoulder.

"Cheer up," said Pete. "I've fallen on a platter lift before." Darren didn't answer.

Pete turned to Yoshi and Kelly. "Now we're going to turn on the skis—a wedge turn."

Darren made a mess of this, too. He skidded and wobbled. He fell. Pete brushed him off. "You just love eating that snow," he said.

They went up the platter lift again. This time Pete

wedge turn: A turn taught to beginner skiers. The skis are positioned in the shape of a wedge with the tips pointed toward each other.

helped Darren on and he made it to the top. "You remember about thinking through your feet," Pete said. Darren nodded glumly. "Now we're going to try to get that weight forward."

Pete grabbed Darren by the arms. "Wrestle the bear!" he said. Darren looked at Pete in astonishment. "Wrestle the bear!" repeated Pete. Halfheartedly, Darren tried to push Pete away. Pete easily shoved him to the right, then to the left.

"Easy meat for this bear," said Pete. "Come on!" he urged. Darren was strong and big for his age. He used his weight now.

"That's more like it," said Pete. Then Darren put all his strength into it.

"Hold it right there!" Pete said. Darren kept his body in the wrestling position. "Where are you?"

Darren looked at his body in relation to his skis. "Forward over the skis," he said.

"Perfect position!" said Pete. "Now, when we turn this time, just wrestle that bear all the way down the mountain."

But before Darren made his first turn, he heard the buzz of a snowmobile. It was Andrea.

"Up to Dome Shelter?" called Pete.

"Just came down," said Andrea. "A couple of the

scientists are up there looking at the instruments."

"Did they say what the lake's doing?" Pete asked.

"Close to 50°C," Andrea said.

Pete tipped back his cap and whistled. "50°! That's high."

"Too high," Andrea agreed. "Lots of steam, too. And they tell me the lake's expanded."

"Wow," said Pete. He looked at the summit. A burst of steam rose above the crater lake, then blew away to the west. "Any seismic activity?" he asked Andrea.

"Grumbles and mumbles, they told me," said Andrea.

Pete frowned and stabbed at the snow with his ski pole. "Looks like Ruapehu might want to spit out a bit of magma before too long. Take care, Andrea."

Andrea revved her snowmobile. "Don't worry—when the big chief speaks, we Maoris listen!"

Kelly watched Andrea go. "I'd love to drive one of those to the top and ski down!"

seismic: Relating to an earthquake.

magma: Hot liquid rock that erupts from a volcano.

Pete shook his head. "No way, Kelly. Your mom told the ski school you were to do nothing but ski and then be at the parking lot at four o'clock every day for her to pick you up."

Kelly made a face at Pete. "She's so anxious! She thinks I could drown every time I brush my teeth." Kelly scowled. "Only-child syndrome—that's my mom! She even makes me wear a red jacket so I can be seen on the mountain! Anyway, you don't need the snowmobile to get to the top. Our motel owner told me you can walk up to the crater lake and ski down."

Pete scratched his chin. "Yeah, it's about ninety minutes walk from the top of the Far West T-bar. Then an awesome ski down. But anyone who goes up there right now, apart from ski patrol and the science guys, is crazy. And you're not allowed anyway."

Kelly shoved out her lower lip. "Meanie."

Pete suddenly jerked his ski poles up. "Action!" he said. "Let's do some beautiful turns on the way down to lunch!"

crater lake: A lake formed at the mouth of the volcano.

T-bar: A ski lift on which two people are pulled up a slope by a T-shaped bar.

Darren's stomach tightened. He'd been working so hard on his skiing that he hadn't realized how hungry he was. But where would he eat?

Yoshi spoke up. "We could have lunch at Ridgetop. They make delicious food."

"Yeah!" said Kelly. "I'm starving!" She turned to Darren. "You coming?" Darren hesitated. He only had five dollars. Kelly seemed to guess his thoughts. She patted her jacket pocket. "Mom's given me heaps," she said. "More than I need."

"All settled then," said Pete. "Follow me down to Ridgetop. When you've finished stuffing your faces, meet me at 1:30 at the ski school. Now, let's make turns Panda Pete can be proud of."

He turned to Darren. "Follow me—and wrestle that bear!"

Pete set off and they all followed in his tracks. Wrestle that bear, Darren told himself fiercely all the way down. His balance improved with every turn.

A t the end of the day, after Yoshi went to Ridgetop, Kelly and Darren skied down to the parking lot. Kelly's mom was waiting for her.

"All right?" she asked Kelly, in a worried tone.

"Stop nagging, Mom."

Kelly introduced Darren. "I was very well behaved," said Kelly. "Wasn't I, Darren?"

Darren decided not to say anything about the way Kelly charged down the slopes or crashed into the ski line. "Very well behaved," he repeated.

Her mom didn't seem convinced. "Make sure she doesn't land herself in trouble up there, Darren." Then she noticed Darren's cracked goggles. "Did you have an accident?" Darren was wondering how to say that he couldn't afford a new pair. Quickly Kelly changed the subject. "Do you want a ride?" she asked.

Darren arrived at Topview to find his mother in the kitchen, beside a mountain of vegetables. There was a pile of potato peels and carrot scrapings on her other side. "Well, how did it go today?" she asked.

"Okay," Darren said. He thought about how he'd wanted to go home in the first hour, before the mist and clouds had cleared. He thought about how he'd wanted his dad to be there. Now he wanted to stay— even though he'd wiped out on the platter lift.

He picked up a peeler. "I'll give you a hand, Mom."

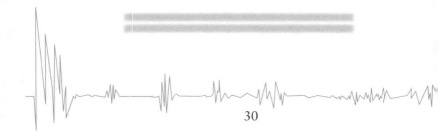

Chapter 3

Darren Goes for a Ride

Fact: Measuring a crater lake's expansion (growth) or contraction (shrinkage) is a way of finding out how close an eruption might be.

AT 8:30 THE NEXT morning, Darren slotted his skis into the rack at the back of the shuttle. The mountain was a mass of snow against a sparkling blue sky.

The shuttle driver, still in his yellow shirt, greeted him. Then he crunched the blue and white bus into gear. It jerked along. "She's slow," Andrea's father said about the bus, "but she's steady."

He chatted to Darren as the shuttle ground its way up the ski road. "My daughter goes to the top of the mountain on one of those buzzy snowmobile things."

He pointed to Ruapehu, gleaming in the sunlight. "*I* wouldn't do that. Might offend the big chief up there, eh? Reckon I'd feel annoyed if people walked all over my head. Never know what might happen. But the young ones—" He didn't finish the sentence and was silent for the rest of the trip.

As the bus rumbled on, Darren thought about Kelly. She loved to go fast, her long hair streaming behind her as she charged down the slope. It was almost dangerous the way she did it, as if she wanted to take risks. Once she lost control and plowed into the ski line, knocking over several skiers.

Pete wasn't amused. "Hey, Kelly. Pete the Panda likes his class to ski in control. Hitting other skiers is a number-one crime." But it didn't take long for Kelly to zoom away again. She just couldn't help it.

The shuttle stopped at the top of the road. Darren got off. His toes, he discovered, were sore after the first day's skiing. He unracked his skis and balanced them on his shoulders. Then he walked to the ski school, remembering to dig the front of his boots into the slippery snow.

He looked at his watch—9:25. Yoshi was already there. He greeted Darren with a smile and introduced Darren to his father, a tall man in glasses.

Mr. Yamada shook Darren's hand. "Yoshi has told me about you. A very good skier, he says."

Darren looked at the ground in embarrassment. "Not as good as Yoshi," he mumbled.

Mr. Yamada raised his right hand. "But Yoshi has skied before." He looked at his watch and gave his son a pat on the back. Then he waved goodbye and walked down to the parking lot.

"My father drives to Auckland today to see Ichiro, my brother," said Yoshi. "Ichiro is in a language school for learning English."

School, thought Darren. With surprise, he realized that he hadn't thought about school at all. A few days ago he thought he would never forget wrestling with Brett. But the mountain had cleared his mind. It was like a huge window letting fresh air into a stuffy room.

Pete came out, wearing sunglasses rather than goggles. "Hi, dynamic duo," he said. "We can't get our terrific three until Kelly arrives."

Kelly rushed up, five minutes late. "Sorry, everybody. Browsing in the ski shop." She noticed Pete's glasses. "Wow! Panda Pete's got cool shades today!"

She pretended to take Pete's photo. Then she grabbed his arm. "Can we go up higher today, nearer the top? Please, please, please?"

"Why not?" Pete said. "Let's take the chairlift to heaven. Click into your bindings and follow me!"

He turned effortlessly down the slope to the open-walled building that housed the rumbling chairlift.

As Yoshi followed Pete, Kelly suddenly thrust a new pair of goggles into Darren's hands. "You're already cracked in the head. You better not be cracked in the goggles, too," she laughed.

Darren was dumbfounded. For him? He couldn't take them. They must have cost at least fifty dollars.

Kelly waved aside his protests. "Dad's got loads of money. No problem. Maybe you can do me a favour some day."

Darren put them on. They fit perfectly. "Great!" said Kelly. She looked at Yoshi and Pete waiting for them. "Hey, let's move!"

dumbfounded: Stunned or surprised.

They skied down in time for the chairlift. It tracked slowly around the building until it was just behind them. "Sit!" said Pete. The chair moved off, carrying them into the air. Pete pulled down the safety bar.

The chair sped up, zooming above the snow. Darren looked at the chair-hook gripping the thick cable above him. Then he looked down at the snow below them. He felt like a bird flying on a wire wing.

The lift went close to soaring cliffs of ice and rock. The cliff walls were so close Darren could almost touch them.

The chair slowed as it approached the landing. Pete pushed up the safety bar. "When you ski off, keep moving and keep your weight forward."

But Kelly cut across Darren's path. Their skis crossed and they tumbled. The next group of skiers fell over them.

Darren was annoyed and embarrassed. He didn't blame Kelly, though. He could hardly say anything when he was wearing those goggles.

Kelly thought it was a huge joke. "Sorry," she giggled. It was as if she found life boring if it went too smoothly. Getting tangled up in the snow, or rushing down a slope out of control—that was exciting to her.

Darren calmed down when he looked at the view. A few light clouds drifted below. But he could see rivers, fields, farms, the glint of small lakes. He could see the rich green woods, a line of forest, a faint trail of smoke from a paper mill. He could even see Topview Motor Inn. Would his mom be looking up at the mountain right now?

"Great to be alive, guys!" said Pete. "Now for some skiing—with a difference."

He pulled two wool gloves from a pocket in his ski jacket and rolled them together. "Let's play ball," he said. "The one with the most points loses—and I'm keeping score."

Kelly's face dropped. "What?"

But Pete was already off. "Come on," he yelled. Darren skied beside him. He caught the gloves Pete threw him, then tossed them to Yoshi—who dropped them. "Yoshi one," said Pete. Yoshi picked up the gloves and tossed them to Kelly—who dropped them. "Kelly one," shouted Pete.

The gloves flew through the air. Everyone leaned forward to catch them. Their skis turned by instinct rather than by thinking. As they reached and turned and caught and threw, they laughed and giggled. They whooped when they'd made a catch and joked when someone else dropped it.

They stopped at the bottom of the slope, chests heaving. "Yoshi two, Kelly four, Darren one," said Pete. Darren took a small bow.

"Teacher's pet," said Kelly. She pushed some snow down the neck of his jacket.

There was the sound of a high-pitched engine buzzing up the slope. "Hey, Pete, it's skiing up here, not football," mocked Andrea.

Kelly eagerly looked at the snowmobile. "Can I have a ride?" Andrea shook her head. "Ski patrol would kill me. Sorry."

A crackling noise came from Andrea's jacket. She pulled out a walkie-talkie and listened intently. "Someone's injured on the Downhill." She took off toward the long wide slopes to the west.

Andrea was back forty minutes later, just as Pete was finishing the lesson. "Only cuts and bruises," she said. "No need for the banana-boat, thank goodness."

"A boat of bananas?" wondered Yoshi.

Andrea laughed. "It's the nickname for the yellow injury sled."

Kelly was impatient to ski down to Ridgetop. "I'm famished! Food! Last one down's a rotten egg!" She skied quickly down the slope.

"I'm going for a quick look around the summit," Andrea said to Pete.

Darren wanted to go. "Can I come?"

Andrea shook her head. "Everyone will want a turn." Yoshi shook his head. "I have had an earthquake. That is enough. No volcano, thank you."

Darren wondered about Yoshi's remark. Had something bad happened to Yoshi during the earthquake at Kobe?

"Okay," said Andrea to Darren. "Just up and back. Don't tell your skiing friend, though!"

Then he was on the back of Andrea's snowmobile. It tracked up the mountain, moving with ease. Up the slopes. Over the bumps. Across the icy patches.

In a few minutes they were far above the skiers. Andrea stopped beside a steel and wood hut. The hut perched on the top of a large rise of snow that overlooked the crater lake.

"Welcome to Dome Shelter,' said Andrea. "It's an emergency shelter for hikers and climbers, but it's got some instruments, too. We leave all that to the scientists. In the middle of winter they have to hack away a few feet of snow and ice to get inside. But it's spring now."

"The lake water's grey," said Darren in surprise.

"A bad sign," said Andrea. "Usually it's blue or green. The old chief is warming up. The mud on the bottom is rising."

Darren looked around. He felt like he was on top of the world. Andrea seemed anxious to get away. "We're inside the level-two zone up here. No sense in hanging around." Just then the lake gave a woof. A burst of steam shot high into the air, passing over their heads. Darren got a whiff of sulphur.

"See what I mean?" said Andrea. Darren hopped on the snowmobile and Andrea drove down.

"I spoke to your dad," said Darren. "He said it wasn't good to go up the mountain."

level-two zone: An area within one and a half kilometres of a volcano crater where no one is allowed.

sulphur: An element often found in natural springs that smells like rotten eggs.

Andrea drove down for a while. Then she throttled back the snowmobile and let it idle for a while. "My dad half-believes the old stories. There's a lot of legend here—like the explanation for how the volcano fires started."

She pointed to a cone-shaped mountain to the east. "Over there is Ngauruhoe. They say that a great Maori priest climbed that mountain one day, just to look over the land. But on the top, a sudden and terrible snowstorm came up. He was so cold that he called to his sisters from way up north to send fire to warm him.

"And they did. They asked the fire demons to send volcanic fire into the mountain. And when it burst out of Ngauruhoe, he was warmed."

She shrugged her shoulders. "I'm sure Pete would have a more scientific explanation."

"Has anyone been hurt by the volcano?" Darren asked.

"About forty years ago the crater lake opened up," said Andrea. "A lahar—a river of mud and water— slid down the mountain, and slammed into a bridge to the south. A few minutes later,

lahar: A flow made of water and volcanic mud.

a train came along and crashed into the river. Over 150 people died. And would you believe it was on Christmas Eve?"

She looked sad thinking about it. "Some people in the town still cry about it. The Tangiwai Disaster."

Andrea pointed to her left, toward the west. "The science guys think that a lahar could run down there."

Darren looked at the skiers turning down the runs on the snowy slopes. "But there's a ski run over there!" he said.

"Lahars don't worry about things like that," said Andrea. She glanced at her watch. "Let's get down to Ridgetop. Your ski friends might have eaten all the food by now!"

She took Darren down to the lodge. As he got off, she said, "Like your new goggles." Then as she buzzed off: "Don't tell anyone where you've been!"

Chapter 4

The Terrible Twitch

B<small>Y THE TIME</small> D<small>ARREN GOT BACK</small> down the mountain, Yoshi had told Kelly about Darren's ride up to the summit on the snowmobile. She was green with envy—almost upset. "That's so unfair!" she said. "I was going to ask you to walk up with me. You owe me a favour."

Darren remembered Yoshi's remark about the earthquake and decided to change the subject. "What was the earthquake like, Yoshi?"

earthquake: Violent movement of the earth's surface.

Immediately, Kelly looked at Yoshi with interest. "Have you been in an earthquake?" Yoshi nodded. "Wow!" said Kelly. "Awesome!"

Yoshi didn't say anything. Kelly caught his mood. "You don't have to talk about it if you don't want to."

"I ski with you," said Yoshi. "So maybe a little."

"It was in Kobe?" Darren asked. "My dad went to Kobe for business once. He liked the buildings."

"Yes," said Yoshi. "Not as big as Tokyo—but very beautiful." He was still for a while, then began talking. "We lived in an apartment in Nagata, a nice part of Kobe. On the third floor. My father and mother and my brother and me—and our little dog Binko."

"Binko," said Kelly. "That's a nice name."

"Yes," said Yoshi. "We were the only family in our apartment block to have a dog. But that night my father was in Tokyo, at a conference for engineers. It was strange, when you think about it. The conference was about saving buildings from earthquakes."

"That's weird," said Kelly.

"And Ichiro—my brother—was sleeping at his school," Yoshi continued. "He was leaving early to go skiing on a class trip. I had to stay because I had a school exam."

"I remember getting up early that morning—my clock radio said about 4:30—because I felt cold. We had gas central heating but my mother used to turn it off when my father was away to save money. When I think about it, turning off that gas was important. When the earthquake came it may have stopped our apartment from catching fire.

"I got up to put an extra blanket over my comforter. But I was still cold. I remember turning on my flashlight—the little camping flashlight I keep beside my bed.

"Then I went to sleep again. I was awakened by Binko. Usually she slept on her mat outside the kitchen until we woke up. But she was scratching at my door and whining. That wasn't like Binko!"

"I got out of bed to let her in. It was so cold! I put on my bathrobe.

"Even when I opened the door, Binko still whined. Her tail was between her legs. Now, of course, I understand. She somehow knew the terrible twitch of the namazu was coming. The twitch that brought the Hanshin Earthquake. The twitch I can never forget."

Kelly frowned. "Yoshi, what's the nam—the nam—whatever you called it."

"In Japanese legend we have a story that earthquakes are caused by the movements of a giant catfish—the namazu. It lives in the mud beneath the surface of the earth," said Yoshi. "And Binko somehow knew."

It rang true, Darren thought. He'd read about animals that had a sixth sense.

"I will never forget the time of the twitch of the namazu. Five forty-six. Five forty-six in the morning, January seventeenth. That was when my world stopped.

"At 5:46, I was bending down to pick up little Binko when our apartment shook and bounced. I was thrown in the air and fell on my knees. I struggled to my feet. I was thrown down again. Our apartment was like a matchbox in a whirlwind.

Kelly listened with her mouth open, fascinated. "How terrible!"

Hanshin Earthquake: Occurred on Tuesday, January 17, 1995, at 5:46 A.M., seriously damaging Kobe City.

"We'd had earthquakes before, but only tiny ones. They were little shivers that sometimes shifted the photos of my grandparents in our living room. Sometimes, the shivers were so weak that only machines could pick them up—the machines the scientists use to measure how strong the earthquake is. What do you call them?"

"Seismographs," said Darren, remembering it from a geography lesson on earthquakes.

"Yes," said Yoshi. "Seismographs. We all knew about earthquakes, though. Mr. Tamose, our teacher, would often have earthquake drills. When he blew his whistle, and yelled 'Jishin!' we would crawl under the desks.

"And he also taught us about the 1923 Great Kanto earthquake. That was when Tokyo and Yokohama lost more than 140 000 people.

seismograph: An instrument that records the force and location of earthquakes.

fault: Crack or fracture in the Earth along which plates of rock move.

"We knew that Kobe was in a place—a line where earthquakes could happen. It is called something special, I think."

"An earthquake fault," said Darren.

"Yes," said Yoshi. "But beautiful Kobe had not had a big earthquake for years," Yoshi went on. "My grandparents remembered one. And Mr. Tamose told us about one that happened hundreds of years ago. My parents could not remember any.

"But this shaking was awful. My books crashed to the floor. My desk fell over. My computer tumbled and the screen smashed. My goldfish bowl flew through the air splashing me with water.

"It seemed to go on forever, but my father told me later it only lasted for about twenty seconds."

"Twenty seconds can be a long time," Darren said. He remembered his seconds with Brett.

"Too long," Yoshi agreed. "My mother yelled out, 'Earthquake, Yoshi! Get under the door.' I knew the drill of Mr. Tamose. Yes, the door frame might protect me. But getting to the door was like riding a wild horse.

"Then everything started tearing and twisting and snapping and sliding. Our home fell down and I fell down, too. Heavy things crashed into my leg and my chest. Then I fell no more.

"The crashing noises stopped. But there were sounds of tinkling glass. When I heard that, I knew I was alive. I tried to call out to my mother. But I couldn't make a noise."

"Why was that?" Kelly asked.

"My computer had fallen on my chest," explained Yoshi. "I managed to push it away. Then I could breathe and call out to my mother. She didn't answer.

"I called again. She moaned. I knew she was badly hurt. But when I tried to get up, I felt much pain in my leg. I touched my leg. My bone was sticking out. I could not move."

Kelly put her hands over her mouth. "Yuk!"

Yoshi looked at Kelly. "It made me feel sick, too. But the worst was that I couldn't help my mother. I cried— even though my father says it is good to be brave.

"I became unconscious. When I woke again, my mother was calling me. Her voice was weak. 'I will not see you again, Yoshi,' she said. 'Be a good boy.' Those were the last words my mother spoke to me."

Yoshi stopped speaking for a few seconds. Kelly put her arm around him and gave him a hug. "That's awful, Yoshi," she said.

Darren thought about his dad—at least he was alive. Darren could see him and talk to him. Then Darren thought about his mom, who was working with his aunt at the motel so he could go skiing. He was lucky.

Kelly spoke again. "What did your dad do?"

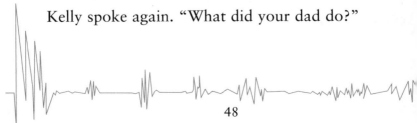

"My father hoped for a miracle and tried to call home—but the lines weren't working. He knew he had to get to Kobe somehow."

"How did he get there?" asked Darren.

"By train, as far as he could. Then people gave him rides in cars," said Yoshi. "He saw what the terrible twitch had done. Houses flattened everywhere. Roads with huge cracks. Bridges lying on top of cars. Trains on their sides.

"Worst of all, he saw smoke and fire. It came from broken electric wires and gas pipes. And it seemed so strange to see fires burning in houses in the snow.

"My father thought we could be trapped in our home, burning to death. He said he felt like screaming.

"When he got to our street, he was stopped by a guard. 'Too dangerous,' the guard said. The guard sent him to a relief centre nearby. It was the school where my brother had spent the night. Many beds were lined up for people to stay. My dad gave his name there. They served him soup and rice, while they checked their list to see if they knew what had happened to us.

"Then he saw my brother. Ichiro was alive—but very tired and shocked. Before the earthquake, my brother had never seen a dead person. But for hours, he had been putting sheets on the gym floor for all of the corpses. There were two hundred bodies lying there for families to identify.

"And every time a body came in, Ichiro thought that it might be my mother or me. Later, my father and brother were allowed to go to our apartment. They saw piles of concrete, timber and smashed glass. Where would they look for us? It was a huge mess. Only motorcycles or motor scooters could get past the bulldozers and the crowds to look for people. And all of the time, there were little earthquakes."

"Aftershocks," said Darren, remembering more of his geography lessons.

"And you were lying there all this time, Yoshi?" asked Kelly.

Yoshi nodded. "For two nights and three days. I could see a little light, so I could tell the days and the nights. My leg throbbed all the time. My chest hurt. I could feel the pain spreading up and down my body. I was so cold. I would have died if I hadn't had my bathrobe. I was hungry. I was thirsty."

aftershocks: *Smaller quakes or shocks that follow the main earthquake.*

"You must have been lonely," said Kelly.

"No, I wasn't," said Yoshi.

Darren guessed why. "Because you had Binko?"

"Yes," smiled Yoshi. "Binko slept beside me. She warmed me. She licked my face. And I was her friend, too. We helped each other.

"Toward the end of the first day, I heard noises and smelled smoke. I will be burned alive, I thought. Then trickles of water ran down the walls and along the floors. The smell of smoke stopped. I dipped my fingers into the water and licked them.

"When the third day came, I knew that I would not live for another day. I could not speak. My leg was very sore. My body was like ice. Then Binko heard something or smelled something. She was so excited. She yelped so hard I thought her head would come off!

"And then I heard an answering bark. My father said later that it came from a sniffer dog. The dog was flown in from Switzerland where it had been trained to use its nose to search for people buried in snow.

"I heard the sound of timber and concrete being taken away, of stones being lifted. Someone pulled away a patch of wall. I could see outside! I could see sky! I was going to live!"

Chapter 5

When Will the Mountain Speak?

Fact: Downhill skiing is also called Alpine skiing. The term *Alpine* comes from *Alps*. The Alps are the mountains in Europe where downhill skiing began.

During the afternoon of the second day, Pete taught them a turn that brought their skis closer together. The skis were easier to turn and glide. And the edges gripped better. Darren wanted to learn more of anything that helped him ski better down the curving slopes and valleys.

Darren noticed that Kelly skied slowly—at first. He thought it was because she was still thinking about Yoshi's story. Finally, she put her foot back on the accelerator. Once again, she was whooshing down the runs and whooping with the thrill of it.

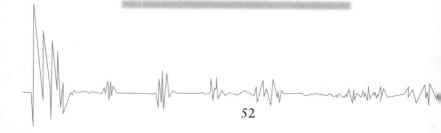

That night, Darren had told his mom about Yoshi's terrible experience. But retelling the story kept him awake for an hour when he went to bed. What if he'd been in an earthquake? Would he be so brave?

The next morning, Darren was glad to see the blue-and-white shuttle coming toward him. He couldn't wait to get up the mountain for his last day of lessons. He wanted to learn everything—and time was running out.

Almost as soon as he sat down, Darren thought again about Yoshi's story. Darren had never been in a horrible disaster, only in a few accidents. Once he'd fallen off his bike on the driveway. He had been chosen for the school soccer team, and he rode home quickly because he couldn't wait to tell his dad. He took the driveway too fast. The pedal had hit the concrete. The tires skidded. In a split second, his knee had hit and scraped along the hard surface.

It had taken him an hour to get the gravel out of his knee. But a bloody knee wasn't like lying for three days in a wrecked building thinking you were going to die.

Darren admired Yoshi's calm. Yoshi seemed wiser

and more mature than Kelly, even though she was probably about two years older. I guess really bad experiences change you, thought Darren.

The shuttle driver broke into Darren's thoughts. "Getting out, young fella? End of the line."

Darren was surprised. Already here! "Sorry." He clumped down the steps, grabbed his skis from the rack, and walked to the ski school area.

He looked at his watch. It was 9:35. Five minutes late. Yoshi would be there. Kelly was always late. But Kelly was there before him, in a dark-blue jacket rather than the red one. She was talking to Pete about something.

"Maybe Andrea shouldn't have taken him up," Pete said. He spoke firmly to her. "Kelly—the mountain's on level-two alert. That means you can't go up." He tapped himself on the chest. "Even I can't go up. So let's stay down here and enjoy skiing."

Kelly made her sad face and pouted her lip. Then she smiled. "Okay, Panda Pete."

"It's good to have adventure," said Yoshi. "But it is good to stay away from danger."

"Couldn't put it better myself, Yoshi," said Pete.

"And Kelly tells me you should know. That was a rough time you had in Kobe. I got into a tricky situation myself a couple of years ago when I got adventure and danger mixed up."

"In skiing?" Yoshi asked.

Pete shook his head. "Nope. A tornado."

"Oooh!" said Kelly. "Let's hear about it!"

"Not now," said Pete. "Maybe later. Right now we've got some serious skiing to do."

They took the chairlift up to Knoll Ridge Café, higher on the mountain than Darren had ever skied. He was surprised by the wind. It was colder than below. The wind blew flurries of snow across the slopes. The snow was icier. The mountain seemed less friendly.

Darren found it harder to balance on his skis. Even Yoshi skidded and seemed uncertain. And Kelly took a tumble.

Pete noticed it. "Let's do something to get our balance right. Let's ski without poles."

Kelly wailed. "No poles! Are you serious?"

Pete held out his gloved hands. "Give them here," he said. He took the poles, skied to the café and left the poles in the ski racks. He skied back, grinning. "Follow me."

Pete turned his skis down the slope and sped off. The others trailed after him. Not having poles worried Darren. He'd found them good for stopping a slide when he stood in line. They helped him get up after a fall. And they felt good in his hands.

But his first three turns amazed him. His body was freer. He could lean forward more easily from the hips. He was wrestling the bear. His skis turned solidly.

Without the poles he could focus on what his feet were doing. He could feel his feet press, then release, press and release as he turned with Pete and Yoshi and Kelly down the run. His heart sang. This was the life. This was the way to go!

All morning they kept at it. They skied new runs, new slopes, different snow. The mountain was always changing, always different.

Darren thought about the ski team at his school. Maybe he could try out for it. If he made it, he'd be able to go skiing again. Maybe his dad would go, too. Darren could show him how well he could ski. To his disappointment, Pete then took them to the top of the chairlift, and handed them their poles. "Time's up, guys."

Kelly wailed, "Your watch is fast."

"When you're having fun, time flies, huh?" said Pete. "Now you guys have lunch and I'll see you at two for our last lesson." He was ready to ski off when Kelly stopped him.

"Have we been good?"

"Yep!" said Pete. "Super good!"

"Then you've got to tell us your story."

"Yes!" said Yoshi.

Pete looked at Darren. "Yes," said Darren.

Pete held his gloves out in surrender. "You win. Let's have something to eat at Yoshi's lodge. Then I'll bore you guys with how I discovered a tornado is no teddy-bear."

Chapter 6
Tickled by a Twister

Fact: A 1925 tornado destroyed four towns in Missouri, Illinois, and Indiana. The tornado covered a distance of 349 kilometres and lasted three-and-a-half hours.

KELLY TOOK A HANDFUL of popcorn. "Now, Panda Pete, tell us all about it."

"Okay," said Pete, "As long as you learn from my little story, Kelly. Adventure's one thing. But looking for danger is plain crazy. Make that double crazy if you're dealing with a tornado."

"Was it in Tornado Alley?" asked Darren, pleased that he remembered another geography lesson.

"Hey!" said Pete. "You've got a good geography teacher at your school. Yep, Tornado Alley is where it happened to me. Missouri—where my folks live— Kansas, Oklahoma, north Texas—that's where these twisters seem to start up.

"I'd just finished a season instructing at Jackson Hole, Wyoming. I figured I might kick back and see the folks before I headed to Ruapehu. And I wanted to show them my pride and joy—a brand-new snowboard."

Yoshi's eyes shone with interest. "A snowboard for a skiing instructor?"

"Yep," said Pete. "Always good to go down the snow in different ways. It keeps me from going stale.

So I drove down from Wyoming. It was early April. It was cold when I left the mountains. The cold air travelled down with me. But when I got to Missouri, I hit a belt of warm weather coming up from the Gulf of Mexico. It was weather that gives you spring fever.

"That's why it's called Tornado Alley—it's a path across the plains where cold air from the north meets warm air from the south." Pete pushed two fingers together to show what he meant. "There was this huge line of cumulonimbus—"

"Excuse me?" said Yoshi.

"No big words, Panda Pete," said Kelly.

"You win," said Pete. "Thunderclouds. The clouds towered so high you could have hidden a hundred skyscrapers in them. All that hot air had no place to go because the cold air made a big wall in front of it. So the hot air just shot straight up.

"Some of those clouds looked bigger than the mountains in Colorado—and boy, they were seething. You could feel the energy. See it. Almost smell it! You just knew it was twister weather."

"Had you been in a tornado before?" Kelly asked.

Pete shook his head. "Nope. But I'd seen the small twisters that form and die in seconds. They just look like a piece of string snaking around and then they're gone. So I wasn't too worried, even by this great heap of clouds. I knew that when the winds inside twisters start spiralling they can go crazy—around 500 hundred kilometres an hour. But I guess I still pictured the baby twisters I'd seen." Pete tapped his head. "No imagination."

"What about your mom and dad?" Darren asked.

"My folks always worried about the danger," Pete said. "Guess they'd listened to Grandpa's stories of the Twister of '25. When he was fifteen, he saw one of the biggest twisters ever. That killer twisted up three states and killed about seven hundred people."

Seven hundred people, thought Darren. That's twice the size of my whole school.

seething: *Constantly moving.*

Pete continued. "And Grandpa told my folks how that twister did terrible things. Stalks of wheat were driven into trees and people. Houses were lifted off the ground. A big train was turned completely around.

"So my folks were prepared—like everyone else in the neighbourhood. They had a special basement under the house, with no windows. And they made sure there was nothing heavy on the floor above it like a freezer or a piano. They kept food, water, and flashlights in it—in case the power went off or the drinking water was ruined.

"But they'd never seen a big twister, either. Living in Tornado Alley doesn't mean worrying about twisters every day of your life. You could live there for years and never see one.

"But that day they didn't like the look of the clouds. There was a dark bulge in the middle of them. It looked like a funnel that you'd pour gasoline down. It was moving and trying to go lower. It was maybe fifteen, twenty kilometres away.

"'Mighty suspicious,' said my dad. 'We'd better turn on the radio. Might be some news.' We didn't have long to wait. The radio said there was a Tornado Watch."

> *Tornado Watch*: A warning that conditions are right for a tornado to form.

"A tornado watch?" said Yoshi. "Everyone watches the tornado?"

Pete chuckled. "No—it's an official warning that the weather could produce tornadoes.

A couple of minutes later, they announced a Tornado Warning. That meant a tornado had hit the ground, and it was starting to do some damage.

"'Get into a safe place,' said the Tornado Warning. Well, I figured that I'd go in my folk's cellar. Couldn't get safer than that. But I wanted to have another peek at this twister. So I went outside the house for a look before I went into the cellar.

"The first thing I noticed was that it was closer. The second thing was that it was more brown than grey now. It was sucking up all the Missouri dirt. Then the cloud where the twister was coming from moved closer to the ground. The twister got thicker. Now it looked like the snout of a huge elephant."

"Like a giant vacuum cleaner?" asked Darren.

Tornado Warning: A warning that a tornado is in the area and that people should take cover.

Pete thought a moment. "Yeah—a vacuum cleaner with a nozzle about two hundred metres wide. And travelling over the ground maybe a hundred kilometres an hour. I saw it move across a farm shed. Whooosh! That shed shattered. Its pieces were sucked up in a swirling mass of dirt and wood and machinery—and anything else that got in that twister's way. About the same time, I started to hear the thing. It was roaring like a couple of speeding freight trains.

"That's when I remembered my new snowboard. I'd left it on the rack on the car! If the twister took it, bang went a month's savings. I figured I had enough time to run to the car and back before the twister got there."

Yoshi considered this for a few seconds. "Very dangerous!"

"Probably. But I'd been watching this thing. Its path was straight. It was going to miss us by maybe three hundred metres. I had plenty of time, I thought."

Pete shook his head. "Big mistake! Tornadoes make their own rules about where they're going. I hightailed it to the car at the end of the driveway, about a hundred and fifty metres away. I unhooked my board and headed for the house. That twister must have seen me. It seemed to bounce off its left leg like a quarterback and came straight for me.

"I took one look at that boiling monster coming

my way and hotfooted it for home. No way did I want to be swallowed up and cut to pieces by half of Missouri's garbage. But the board was slowing me down.

"I decided the board had to go. I dropped it and headed for the house. But I'd only gone about twenty metres when I realized I wasn't going to make it back to the cellar. I was too slow and too late."

Darren's throat felt dry. He swallowed. "What did you do?"

Pete smiled thinly as he thought about it. "I dived headfirst into the end of some big pipes that my dad was putting together to water his crops."

"But you said a big twister lifted a train," said Yoshi. "A pipe, even a big pipe, would be no good!"

Pete shrugged his shoulders. "Right, Yoshi. If the twister had sucked up that pipe, I would have been dead as a doornail. But it seemed better than just lying in the open. It gets worse.

"As I dived into the pipe, I looked up and saw my mom staring at me through the window. Her eyes were as wide as headlights. She'd been worried about me and hadn't gone to the cellar yet. I remember thinking that I'd not only gotten myself into a big mess. I'd gotten my mom there, too."

"But you lived, Panda Pete!" said Kelly. "That

nasty twister didn't get you."

"Yeah," Pete agreed. "The thing screamed by me as if the end of the world was coming. Then it all went quiet. I crawled out a few minutes later. The twister had sidestepped again. It missed me and the pipe by about fifteen metres. Too darn close!"

"Was the house damaged?" said Darren.

"Nope," said Pete. "A clean miss. But I never saw my board again. It must have gone up so high some old weather god is probably riding it in the sky somewhere. And my car was picked up and dumped a hundred metres away. Totalled!"

Yoshi's face looked more serious than ever. "You were very lucky!"

Pete nodded. "Twice lucky. When all the dust had settled, something made me look back inside that pipe. There was a big rattlesnake in it. It must have been about one metre from my head."

Kelly opened her mouth and shut her eyes. "A rattlesnake! My worst nightmare!"

Pete grinned. "Guess it was so scared by the twister, same as me, that it forgot to strike." He glanced at his watch and suddenly stood up. "See you, champs. Two o'clock outside the ski school for our last lesson." He walked outside and clicked into his bindings. He gave them a thumbs-up and was gone.

"Two o'clock," Kelly said. "That's two hours away." Her eyes widened with a daring thought. "We've got time to walk to the top. Let's do it!"

Yoshi shook his head firmly. "No," he said. "Too dangerous!"

"Darren?" asked Kelly. "You owe me a favour, remember."

Those goggles, Darren thought. He was grateful for Kelly's kindness. But he wanted to ski rather than waste precious time trudging up for a view he'd already seen. And Pete had told them not to go.

"I want to ski," he said.

"Me, too," said Yoshi. Kelly rolled her eyes.

"Wimps!" She stuffed the last of the popcorn in her mouth. "Join you in a couple of minutes."

Darren and Yoshi clicked into their skis.

"Kelly likes danger," said Yoshi.

Darren thought about that. *Did* Kelly like risks? Maybe she did the opposite thing whenever her mom told her to be careful—like he often did. But did that mean she liked danger?

By 2:15, Kelly was not only in Darren's thoughts, but also in Yoshi's and Pete's. She hadn't showed up for the lesson!

Pete was puzzled. "Kelly okay? Did she say she was going anywhere?" Darren and Yoshi couldn't answer.

The last lesson started. Pete tried hard to make it interesting and fun. But without Kelly it wasn't the same. And Pete seemed concerned. He looked around the field as if expecting Kelly to show up and join the class. Not even a cheery remark from Andrea as she buzzed past on her snowmobile could make him laugh.

On the other side of the mountain, a woman was talking to the garage attendant as he filled her new four-wheel-drive vehicle with gas.

"I'm picking up my daughter from a ski class soon," said the woman. "Then we're flying back to Sydney."

Suddenly, her jaw dropped. The garage attendant swivelled to look at what had hypnotized the woman.

"Oh, my God," he gasped.

The woman jumped into the car and roared off. The big tires squealed.

A grey-brown cloud was pushing up from the top of the mountain. It surged higher and higher, bulging and blasting into the air. In a few seconds, it towered into the sky—seething, twisting, boiling.

The big chief with fire in his belly was speaking.

Ruapehu had erupted.

Chapter 7
Missing

Fact: When Ruapehu erupted at 4:50 p.m. on September 23, 1995, the lifts had closed for the day. Most of the skiers were off the mountain or lower down on the mountain.

DARREN, YOSHI, AND PETE gazed open-mouthed at the clouds hurtling up from the mountain. They flew upward like rockets, surging and belching higher and higher.

Lava bombs shot hundreds of metres into the air, trailing smoke and steam tracers as they thudded onto the snow. Darren's heart thumped when he realized that they were falling where he'd been the previous day with Andrea.

A river of mud and debris began flowing over the side of the crater, snaking a dark highway in the

> **lava bombs**: Molten rocks hurled into the air by an erupting volcano that cool and land as solid shapes.

snow. Lahar! Darren remembered Andrea's words. It was travelling the route she'd pointed out to him.

"I hope the skiers there have packed up for the day," said Pete. "That lahar's probably travelling about sixty kilometres an hour."

The clouds soared higher. In only a few seconds, they had risen up thousands of metres. Pete was awed. "The power!" he murmured. He turned away from the magnetic sight, looking at Darren and Yoshi.

"End of skiing for the season, I guess. You guys were great. But you'd better get off the mountain now. And Yoshi—get your stuff from Ridgetop and go down with Darren." He turned to go.

"What about Kelly?" asked Darren.

"Maybe at Ridgetop?" Pete flung over his shoulder as he skied off. He looked purposeful and busy, a professional with an emergency to attend to.

Darren stared at the mountain again. The grey-brown clouds were thicker and stronger than before, pouring into a darkening sky. Parts of the mountain were smudged, as if a giant had pressed a dirty hand into the snow.

"We'd better look for Kelly," Darren said to Yoshi.

"She is not in Ridgetop," said Yoshi.

"How about the café?" Darren asked.

They joined hundreds of skiers slowly making their way downhill. Children were crying. Gloves and hats were lying in the snow. Some skiers were in the way. Darren fell twice as he tried to avoid skiers who had stopped in the middle of the run to gape at the eruption. Even Yoshi fell once.

At the café they took off their skis and clumped inside. It was deserted. Darren approached the white-aproned woman behind the counter. She was staring at the eruption through the window. "Have you seen a skier in a red jacket?" he asked.

"A dark-blue jacket," Yoshi corrected.

"She's about fourteen and—"

The woman interrupted Darren. "Sorry." She didn't even turn around.

Darren and Yoshi walked out of the café. Darren wondered if Kelly was sick. Or she might have hurt herself skiing down to them for the lesson. Darren felt the bruise on his hip where he'd fallen on the first day. Falling was easy enough to do, especially when you skied as fast as Kelly did.

They went to the first-aid room. There were four people needing help. A young snowboarder was lying down, holding a broken wrist. A mother with her wheezing daughter was asking if anyone had handed in an asthma inhaler. And a middle-aged man with blood on his jacket was having a bandage put on a cut on his forehead.

But there was no Kelly. And the two medical staff—a bearded doctor and a no-nonsense nurse—couldn't remember anyone like Kelly coming in that afternoon. "Guess she's gone home. You'd be wise to do the same," said the nurse briskly. She turned back to the snowboarder.

"Maybe she's at the parking lot," Darren said to Yoshi as they walked out.

"Waiting for her mom?"

Yoshi shrugged his shoulders but he walked with Darren to the parking lot.

There were cars everywhere. The parking attendants were waving them on. "Please go down to lower ground. Please leave the parking area!"

But nobody was listening. Anxious drivers wouldn't leave until they'd found their families. Others were so fascinated by the belching clouds that they ignored the horns and flashing headlights of the cars behind them.

briskly: Quickly.

It's a mess, thought Darren. Just like a busy bridge when

72

somebody breaks down. Then he and Yoshi saw Kelly's mother in her four-wheel drive.

Darren ran between the cars and tapped on the window. Kelly's mom rolled down the window, staring blankly at Darren. She looked worried. "Yes?"

Then she remembered. "You're the boy who's skiing with Kelly," she said eagerly. "Is everything all right? Is Kelly with you?" The words rushed out.

She gazed at Darren expectantly. Then her eyes darted away to take in another horrified look at Ruapehu's towering clouds. Darren didn't know what to say. Then he stammered. "Maybe Kelly's still skiing." Mrs. Gale's eyes flashed back to Darren.

"What!" she said. "Isn't she with you?" Her face seemed to collapse. She put her head in her hands and moaned.

"I'll go and look for her," Darren said. Kelly's mom shook her head in doubt. "Can you do that? Will they let you up the mountain?"

Gee, thought Darren. She's right. We won't be able to use the lifts. "Maybe she's waiting at the ski school," he said.

Mrs. Gale clutched Darren's arm. "Look, you tell Kelly I'm waiting. Tell her I want her down—now!"

Darren's mind raced. How do you find someone who's not in any of the places she should be?

He walked quickly back to Yoshi. "Kelly's mom wants us to find her." He looked at the mountain pouring out clouds and fumes. It was hopeless.

Yoshi spoke quietly. "I think I know where she is." Darren's head jerked back to Yoshi. Relief mixed with fear. "Where?"

Yoshi spoke again. His voice and face were serious, his eyes steady. "I think Kelly has walked to the top of the mountain. She wanted to go there very much. I think she went there after lunch." He turned to look at the billowing mass erupting from the cone of the mountain. "I think she's up there."

Darren's fear sharpened. Yoshi's words were like a light being switched on. Kelly had always wanted to go to the top of the mountain. She'd been jealous of him when she found out he'd gone to Dome Shelter on the back of Andrea's snowmobile.

She had pestered Pete to take her to the top. She would have remembered Pete's words the first day of skiing. He had said it was about a ninety-minute walk from the top of the Far West T-bar. Then an awesome ski down.

billowing: Rising in masses.

Pete hadn't taken them over to the Far West T-bar, but that wouldn't have bothered Kelly. She'd have looked at her trail map, hopped on the T-bar alone, gone to the top, and then walked up. She would have ignored Pete's warning. That was Kelly!

Darren and Yoshi grabbed their skis and ran to the chairlift. The chairlift attendant waved them away. "Are you crazy? In case you haven't noticed, this mountain's erupting! We have a level-five alert here. We're only downloading. Get off the mountain!"

Darren protested. "We've got a friend who might be up there." The attendant wasn't interested. "Talk to the Ski Patrol, pal! Then get out before this thing blows up completely!"

Darren and Yoshi ran to the Ski Patrol office. They were about to knock on the door when Andrea buzzed to a stop on her snowmobile.

Darren shouted to her. "We can't find Kelly anywhere. We're sure that she's up on the mountain somewhere!"

Andrea left the snowmobile idling while she walked over, worried.

level-five alert: The highest eruption alert for a large and dangerous eruption.

idling: Running but not in use.

75

"How sure?"

Darren felt silly when he tried to explain. "She wasn't at the lesson. And we can't see her anywhere. And—uh—her mom doesn't know where she is."

Andrea listened. "But are you sure?" Darren and Yoshi said nothing. "One of the patrollers has just swept the area up there," said Andrea. "They found nothing but lava bombs and melting snow. Not a skier anywhere."

She put her hand on Darren's shoulder. "Look, Darren. I think you'll find that Kelly's gone down without your knowing." Darren looked doubtful. Andrea's voice firmed. "Darren! Believe me. Now I've got work to do. And you and Yoshi should get off the big chief before he gets you." She walked into the Ski Patrol office.

"Kelly is up there," said Yoshi solemnly. "I feel it in my heart."

Darren looked toward the mountain just as a huge cloud billowed up so high it towered over the others. There was no doubt about it. The eruption was getting worse.

Everyone said the boys should leave. Andrea, the parking lot attendant, the guy at the chairlift, Pete, and the first-aid nurse had told them that.

Darren knew he and Yoshi should do what they

were told and get off the mountain. Yoshi should go back to his father. The Kobe earthquake had been bad enough. Why look for more trouble? And he should get into the shuttle and go down to Topview. His mom would be worried.

That was the sensible thing to do. But he felt bad about leaving Kelly, especially when Kelly had given him the goggles. And she'd asked him to go up with her as a favour. Maybe if he'd gone with her she might not be lost. But he could do nothing. There was no way up.

Out of nowhere a picture flashed into his mind. It was of his dad storming out of Mrs. Ramsey's office, slamming the door, gunning his car and taking off in a squeal of tires.

Immediately an idea came to him, like a match flaring into flame. But it was such a daring idea that his heart raced. His knees shook.

People would try to stop him. Plus, Kelly was probably not there anyway, whatever Yoshi thought. Plus, he wouldn't have the nerve. Plus, it was stupid. Plus, it was dangerous. Plus, he—

He ran to the snowmobile and jumped on. He gripped the thumb-throttle the way he'd seen Andrea do. He twisted the button. The engine revved up. The tracks bit into the snow. The snowmobile moved. He was off.

As Darren started up the slope toward the Far West T-bar, a startled "Hey!" came from Andrea as she rushed out of the Ski Patrol office.

At the same time, someone jumped into the space behind him on the snowmobile. It rocked. A pair of skis jabbed him in the back.

"I'm coming, too," Yoshi said.

Chapter 8
Hold On!

Fact: The 1995 eruption of Ruapehu was the largest in fifty years. In eighteen days, the eruption completely emptied the crater lake of about seven million tonnes of water.

Darren went slowly to begin with. Above all, he had to get to where Kelly might be. And he'd never driven a snowmobile before.

But it was easier than he thought, even though the machine bumped over rough snow. On a day of sunshine, snow, and play, it would have been fun. He used more throttle to get up the steeper slopes. He made sure to go directly up the fall-line, rather than trying to climb at a sideways angle. Whatever happened, he couldn't let the snowmobile roll over.

> **throttle**: _Lever or pedal for controlling the flow of fuel._
>
> **fall-line**: _The natural downhill course between two points on a slope._

They moved west as they climbed. Yoshi pointed out the direction from his trail map. From the bottom of the mountain the eruption clouds had looked big enough. From closer up, they staggered Darren with their size.

They looked as solid as soup with their mixture of gas, ash, steaming and boiling water, and bits of rock. Whatever the soup was made of, Darren didn't like the look of it.

They climbed higher. Yoshi pointed to an area about one hundred and eighty metres up and ahead of them. The snow was spotted with dark pieces of rock. And beyond that was the "stained road" where the river of mud had flowed down from the crater lake.

Darren throttled back. They were in the rock-dotted area now. He steered carefully and slowly. The first lava rocks were small—fist-size. But, higher up, they were larger—the size of a backpack, of a freezer, even of a small car. Some were still steaming.

"Very dangerous," said Yoshi. Darren nodded. The crater was at least two kilometres away. He was awed by the power that could hurl rocks that distance. And he and Yoshi were right in the line of

lava rocks: Rocks formed when molten lava is thrown into the air by an erupting volcano.

fire! If even a fist-size rock hit his head—he wished he was wearing his bicycle helmet.

They guessed that they were close to where Kelly would be if she had decided to walk up. Yoshi gripped Darren's arm. "Over there!" Darren followed the line of Yoshi's outstretched arm. At first he couldn't see anything. He strained his eyes.

About three hundred metres further up, he thought he saw something dark blue lying in the snow. The colour looked so much like a rock. It was no wonder the ski patroller had missed it. If Kelly had worn her red jacket, maybe she would have been seen more easily. But it was definitely there and definitely a human shape. It had to be Kelly!

The snowmobile was hitting almost as much rock as snow. It was slow going. They got off and started to run.

There was a gigantic blast from the crater. "The sky!" Yoshi yelled. Darren looked up in horror. There were dozens of black spots above them trailing steam. Then the spots turned into rocks, a waterfall of rocks—heading straight for them.

Darren and Yoshi hit the ground and hugged the snow. They curled up as tightly as they could, arms over their heads. Rocks and choking ash splattered around them.

Darren realized that this was what had happened

to Kelly. She'd been struck by black lightning—rocks from the sky. And now the mountain's out to get all of us, he thought.

The rocks slowly stopped thudding into the snow. Darren cautiously opened his eyes. Two metres away was a rock bigger than his school desk, steaming in the melting snow. Yoshi's face was pale. He knew they shouldn't be there.

They'd been lucky—but the snowmobile hadn't. It was under a hissing rock, smashed and useless.

A cloud swirled over them, then floated away. But it was enough to sting Darren's eyes and throat. He felt dizzy and had to drop to his knees. Gas!

"Wet handkerchief," Yoshi yelled. He soaked his handkerchief in the snow, then put it over his nose and mouth. Darren fumbled for his handkerchief in his pocket and did the same. The dizzy feeling passed. But his throat still felt raw.

They looked to where Kelly had been. She'd gotten up and was stumbling toward them. She was shaky and looked like she had a concussion. Still, she managed a smile.

concussion: *Stunned reaction caused by a hard blow to the head.*

Darren was working on how to get Kelly quickly to safety without a snowmobile.

Suddenly, Yoshi pointed up the mountain and screamed at her. "Look out!"

A river of mud, ash, and ice had breached the crater lake wall and was sloshing down the mountain. It came with the speed of a racing skier. And Kelly was right in its path.

Kelly shakily turned her head. The thick wave rolled toward her. She tried to run but was too slow. The wave sent her sprawling. She tumbled over and over. Darren and Yoshi watched helplessly as the lahar swirled toward a rocky bluff. It spilled over the bluff and took Kelly with it.

They scrambled to the edge of the bluff and looked over. Below was a sickening fifteen-metre drop to a bed of splintered rocks, snow, and oozing mud.

But Kelly wasn't lying broken and dead on the snow below. Somehow she'd thrown out her arms to grip a rock a metre below the lip of the bluff. One knee was on a small outcrop another metre down. The other dangled in space. Her hair, face, and jacket were coated in grey mud.

"Help me," she said. Her eyes were wide with terror. Darren and Yoshi tore off their gloves and leaned over as far as they could. They gripped Kelly's arms but they couldn't pull her up.

bluff: A cliff.

Darren wondered if he could climb over and push Kelly up. But the bluff was so slippery with mud that it would be a shortcut to an early grave.

Darren knew they needed help. He was stronger, but Yoshi was a better skier. He should stay, holding on to Kelly. Yoshi should ski down. "Get help, Yoshi," Darren said. Yoshi didn't argue. He got to his feet and was gone.

Darren lay on the dirty mixture of snow and mud, his head over the side of the bluff. His body shivered as the cold and wet soaked through his clothes. The mud got into his mouth. It tasted bitter and acidic. But he didn't let go of Kelly.

Time passed in slow-motion agony as he held on with his right arm. He braced against the lip of the bluff with his left to keep himself from sliding over.

"Hold on," said Kelly. "Please hold on."

For a few minutes, Darren encouraged Kelly. "They'll be back soon. Everything'll be fine." But soon even talking was taking precious energy. Darren stopped speaking, willing himself to hold on. His shoulder joint and wrist burned with the effort. Kelly didn't say anything, either.

Again the picture of his dad storming out of Mrs. Ramsey's office came into his mind. But he wasn't going to run away. He was cold and muddy, scared and aching. But he was going to hold on. Hold on. Hold on.

Darren's wrist hurt so much he thought it would break. His hand was freezing. Worst of all, he felt himself slipping, slowly but surely, to the edge. If he kept holding on to Kelly, in a few minutes he would go over, too.

That was when Kelly spoke. Her voice was strong and calm, as if she'd made up her mind about something. "You're going to fall over the edge if you hold me any longer."

Darren didn't answer.

Kelly spoke again, more clearly. "This is my fault.

I'm sorry." She was silent for a few seconds. Then she said, "Darren, I'm going to count to ten. Then I'll let myself drop. Don't stop me."

The thought horrified Darren. "No!"

"Yes," said Kelly. There was a pause. "One." Another pause. "Two." Another pause. "Three."

"No!" said Darren. "You'll be all right. They'll be here any minute." The pain in his arm was agonizing. He slid closer to the edge.

"No, they won't," said Kelly. "Yoshi probably didn't get down." A pause. "Four." Darren held on.

"Five." He hated hearing her say the numbers. Each one was like a bell tolling for a funeral. What Kelly said to Pete when she was late the first day— "I'll probably be late for my own funeral."—flashed through his mind.

"Six. Seven." A pause. "Eight. Nine."

Another pause. "I mean it," said Kelly. "I'm going to say ten. Then I'll let myself drop." Darren knew that he wouldn't be able to hold Kelly if she let go.

The cold seeped through him. His body shivered. He thought of the way he and Yoshi had searched for Kelly, of the risks they'd taken. He thought of the dangers they'd faced. He recalled how his mom had given him this vacation. Everything would be ruined if Kelly did what she said she was going to do. Anger swept over him. No way!

He yelled at Kelly so hard his voice cracked. "I'm not letting go! If you drop, I drop. So shut up and hang on!" Darren's anger gave him strength. He gripped even harder with his right arm. He pushed harder at the rock with his left.

Kelly made a noise between a sob and a laugh. "Meanie," Kelly said.

Just then Darren heard the buzz of snowmobiles.

"Hold tight!" said a voice. It was Pete. He reached over Darren and grabbed Kelly. "Move away, Darren," he ordered. Darren crawled back and collapsed on the snow.

He watched as Andrea plunged an ice axe into the snow, tied a rope to it, then tied it to herself. Her actions were fast yet controlled.

"Anchor me, Dad," Andrea said.

Andrea's father was there. Now he was in a long yellow jacket. He grabbed the ice axe, and he braced himself. He looked big and strong enough to hold a herd of elephants.

Calmly but quickly, Andrea lowered herself over the bluff and onto the knob beside Kelly. "Now!" she shouted. She shoved Kelly upward and Pete did the rest. Kelly came over the lip of the bluff and lay on the snow. "I'm sorry," she sobbed.

But Andrea, her father, and Pete weren't listening to apologies. "Hurry!" said Andrea. Kelly flopped on the back of Andrea's snowmobile. Darren climbed onto the snowmobile that Andrea's father was driving. Pete clicked into his skis and skied down behind the snowmobiles.

In a minute, they were all out of the danger zone. Darren looked back at the mountain. A shower of rocks was falling on the slopes they'd just left. They'd escaped—but barely.

anchor: To hold in place; to act as an anchor for someone.

knob: A rounded hill.

Darren's right arm ached. His whole body trembled. Yet his mind was clear. He and Yoshi had done the right thing.

Darren knew that he would always remember this day.

Nobody spoke until they stopped outside the Ski Patrol office where Yoshi was waiting anxiously. When he saw them, his smile spread from ear to ear.

Andrea and Pete helped Kelly into the first aid centre. Darren guessed that Mrs. Gale would be there, almost hysterical.

Andrea's dad came over to Darren and gave him a bear hug. It hurt—but Darren didn't mind.

"Proud to know ya, son!" Then he chuckled. "I came to find Andrea. Then she told me I was heading up the mountain on those little buzzy things! Guess my daughter got her old man up the big chief at last, eh?"

Pete came back from first aid and went over to Darren. "Great job," he said. "You're a hero. We're all proud of you and Yoshi. Come down to first aid and we'll check you out."

He patted him on the shoulder. Darren winced again. "Think you're strong enough to take a few words of thanks from Kelly's mom?" Pete asked. "She's mighty anxious to see you. Then Andrea's dad will get you and Yoshi down to Topview."

He spoke to Yoshi. "Think you should call your dad from here? Tell him you're okay?" Yoshi nodded.

Darren and Yoshi walked down with Pete. Darren felt weak and ravenous at the same time. What he'd give for a hamburger! And he looked forward to getting rid of all the mud in a hot shower.

But first he wanted to see Kelly. He wanted to tell her everything was all right. Then he was going to tell his mom all about it. Then he'd be going back home to his school, to his class, to his teachers, to the principal.

But before that he would say goodbye to Yoshi and Kelly—and Pete. Then they would return to their homes. Would he see them again? Or see Andrea? Or have another ride with her dad in his chugging shuttle bus?

wince: To shrink back in pain.

ravenous: Very hungry.

Darren would be going back to his home and to a dad who wouldn't be living there. Before he'd gone to the mountain, he'd wanted his dad to come back.

Now he knew his dad would not be coming home.

Yet the thought didn't make him feel sick and tight in the chest anymore. It was strange. The mountain had taken him out of his troubles. But it had helped him face up to them too.

Dad would be living somewhere else. But now it wasn't the end of the world.

As Pete opened the door of the first-aid shed for Yoshi and Darren, Darren looked up again at Ruapehu. The clouds poured from the mountain more thickly than ever, rolling massively to the sky. It's your turn now, big chief, thought Darren.

But I'll be back.

Earth Facts

Lava flows are streams of molten rock from a volcanic crater or vent. The molten rock has been heated to temperatures between 800° –1200° C.

"Level alerts" are levels of eruption warning, from zero, indicating no volcanic activity, to five, indicating a large and dangerous eruption.

Eruption clouds are a column of gases, ash, and rock fragments. (The Ruapehu eruption pushed clouds up to twelve kilometres into the sky.)

During the 1995 eruption of Ruapehu, fine, light ash covered the central part of the North Island, closing airfields and stopping nighttime flights.

A lava bomb can be as small as a golf ball or as big as a car and weigh several tonnes. Large lava bombs can cause damage by destroying homes, property, and wiping out trees.

The Pinatubo eruption in the Philippines, was one of the world's biggest. It thrust eruption clouds about nineteen kilometres into the air. The ash reached the stratosphere and then circled the globe, causing climate changes in some countries for weeks or longer.

Ruapehu erupted again in June 1996, after months of inactivity, forcing the ski areas to close down once more. It has stayed quiet in 1997 and 1998 and most scientists now believe it will not erupt for another 50 to 100 years.

Although most tornadoes in North America move in a northeasterly direction, they sometimes make u-turns, or even complete circles. They can also lift off the ground to resettle a few metres further on, leaving one house untouched but destroying the house next to it.

Cumulonimbus clouds are masses of clouds that rise up like mountains. It is the formation present in the sky in thunderstorm weather.

Scientists use the Richter scale to indicate the strength of an earthquake: 2.5 is very weak, while 9.5 is total destruction. The Kobe earthquake measured 7.2 on the Richter scale.

Where to from Here?

You've just read the story of Darren's violent meeting with a volcano. Here are some ideas for finding more stories about people dealing with disasters.

The Library

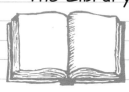

Some books you might enjoy include:
- *Out of the Dust*, by Karen Hesse
- *Climb or Die*, by Edward Myers
- *Night of the Twisters*, by Ivy Ruckman

Here's a non-fiction book to try:
- *Volcanoes*, by Neil Morris

TV, Film, and Video

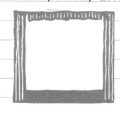

Check TV listings and ask at a video store or your library for films about natural disasters.

The Internet

Try key words such as *volcano, natural disasters, hurricanes, tornadoes,* and *earthquakes.* The Environment Canada site, *www.ec.gc.ca,* is a great source for information about storm disasters.

People and Places

Ask family and friends if they have ever experienced floods, earthquakes or other natural disasters. If so, how did they cope? What stories do they have to tell?

The Ultimate Non-Fiction Book

Be sure to check out the companion volume to *Edge of Disaster. Earth Alert* tells you facts about past natural disasters and tells you what it is like to live through them.

Decide for yourself
where fiction stops
and fact begins.